When there was a ballet

www.roobarbandcustard.tv © 1974-2009 A&B TV limited. All rights reserved. Roobarb & Custard created by Grange Calveley.

© Mogzilla 2010 www.mogzilla.co.uk/roobarbandcustard ISBN: 978-1-906132-13-2 Printed in Malta. 5 4 3 2 1

It was a bitterly cold afternoon. Roobarb and Custard shivered in the wind and snow as they trecked across the garden.

Moggy and Princess had been holding an evening singing session, but their voices were whisked away by the wind.

'It's not fit for a dog to be out,' Custard grumbled.
'Nonsense!' said Roobarb. 'This chilly weather means tomorrow's conditions should be perfect for my spectacular ballet-on-ice!'

'Eh?' said a frosty Custard.

'I'm planning a special performance of Duckpond on Ice,'

declared Roobarb, 'and rehearsals have already begun!'

With that, he twirled off.

First thing next morning, Roobarb raised his weather-forecast gear into the sky.
Results: H2O=freezing.

Everyone helped to prepare for the show.

Post Dog's dogsbodies set out chairs,

while the birds practiced their acrobatics.

Meanwhile, Moggy ran through her scales, and Poodle Princess howled 'red lorry, yellow lorry, red lorry, yellow lorry.'

At 7 o'clock, the lights were lit and the crowds arrived. Everything was ready.

'I announce this ballet-on-ice... open!'

trilled Poodle Princess. But her voice was drowned out by Moggy's opening aria.

Custard, as Dame Mange Blancmange, gave a thumping pas du chat onto the ice. Rover, as the Prince, skated over, bowing low.

With a skillful pirouette, he span Custard far too fast.

But Custard had stage-fright, and stood frozen to the spot.

Suddenly, out of the wings, the birds pushed their way to the front of the stage.

They began to show off their stupefying balancing act, perlious plate-spinning and death-defying sumersaults... on ice!

The audience loved it. They applauded loudly as the birds jumped and span. Everyone agreed that this was proper entertainment.

Rover skated on, but there was nothing he could do. Custard was still frozen, and the birds had stolen the show.

As the birds took bow after bow, Custard and Rover slid off-stage in a dramatic huff.

'What a performance!' sighed Mouse.
'I wish this evening would never end!'

'It'll have to soon,' said Roobarb,

'This pond has a crack in it.'

As Roobarb went up to take his bow, the ice gave in with a tremendous

CRACK !

And finally...
Poodle Princess got a word in:

'The end!'

More marvellous adventures with Roobarb & Custard!

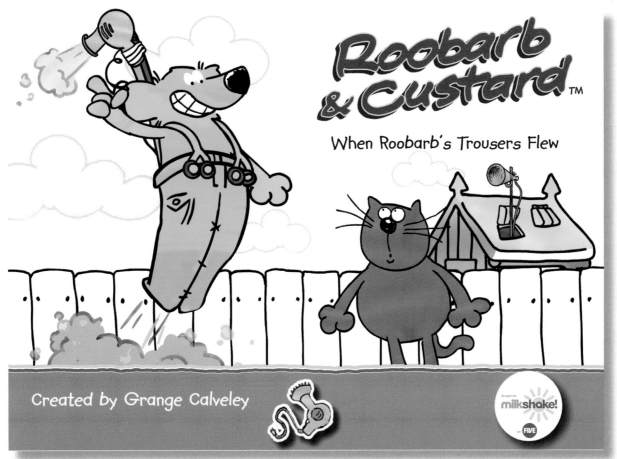

Roobarb & Custard™

When Roobarb's Trousers Flew

Created by Grange Calveley

When Roobarb's trousers flew
ISBN: 978-1-906132-14-9

Bag yourself more Roobarb & Custard books online at

www.mogzilla.co.uk/shop

Roobarb & Custard™

When there was a pottery party

Created by Grange Calveley

As seen on milkshake! on FIVE

When there was a pottery party
ISBN: 978-1-906132-12-5

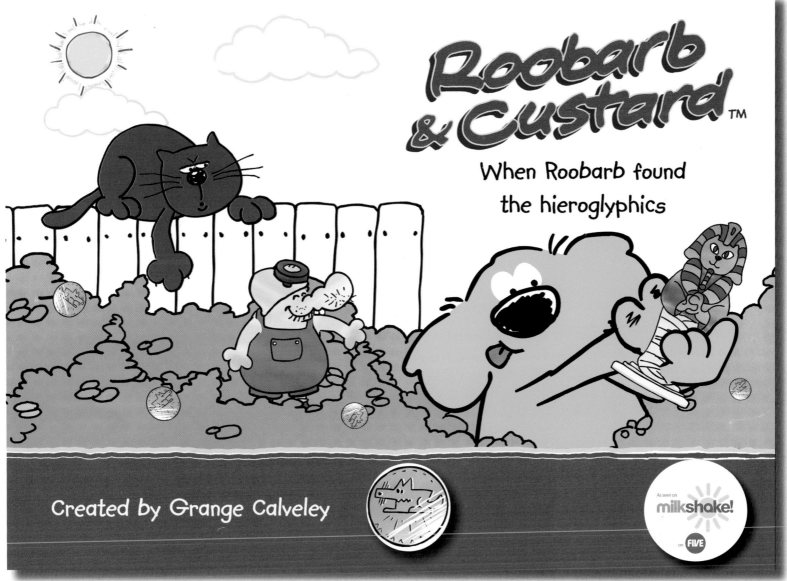

Roobarb & Custard™

When Roobarb found the hieroglyphics

Created by Grange Calveley

When Roobarb's found the hieroglyphics
ISBN: 978-1-906132-11-8